ELLA & MRS GOOSEBERRY

To Scotty for his everlasting love.
To my mother and Sofie for giving
me my writing wings.

– V.C.

Especially for my Mum, Nan Peg and
Granny Gran. Thank you for always
knowing where to find love.

– P.P.

First published 2019

EK Books
an imprint of Exisle Publishing Pty Ltd
PO Box 864, Chatswood, NSW 2057, Australia
226 High Street, Dunedin, 9016, New Zealand
www.ekbooks.org

Copyright © 2019 in text: Vikki Conley
Copyright © 2019 in illustrations: Penelope Pratley

Vikki Conley & Penelope Pratley assert the moral right to be
identified as the creators of this work.

A CiP record for this book is available from the National
Library of Australia.

ISBN 978-1-925335-25-5

Designed by Big Cat Design
Typeset in Minya Nouvelle 18/28pt
Printed in China

This book uses paper sourced under ISO 14001 guidelines
from well-managed forests and other controlled sources.

10 9 8 7 6 5 4 3 2 1

ELLA & MRS GOOSEBERRY

DISCOVERING WHAT LOVE LOOKS LIKE

Vikki Conley & Penelope Pratley

Ella lived next door
to Mrs Gooseberry.

Mrs Gooseberry
always slammed
her door.

Sometimes Ella peeked from her bedroom at Mrs Gooseberry in her backyard.

Mrs Gooseberry would pick tomatoes. She would collect some eggs. She would talk to her chickens.

'Why is Mrs Gooseberry grumpy in her front yard, and happy in her backyard?' said Ella.

'Mrs Gooseberry has lost her love.
She gets sad and lonely,' said Ella's mother.

'Her husband was very old.
Now she has only her
vegetables and her chickens.'

Ella didn't know that
you could lose love.

She wondered if lost
love could be found.

That afternoon, Ella did some baking.

'What does love look like?' she said to her mother, who had flour on her cheek and dough on her nose.

'It's warm, like a home-cooked pie,' said Ella's mother. 'It makes your tummy warm from the inside.'

After school, Ella stayed behind to help.

'What does love look like?' she asked her teacher, who had glitter in her hair and paint on her clothes.

'It's like lanterns in the night,' said Ella's teacher. 'Sparkly and bright.'

At dancing lessons, Ella waited for everyone to leave.

'What does love look like?' she asked her dance teacher, who had arms stretched wide and one foot in the air.

'It's like a bird,' said
Ella's dance teacher.
'It makes you sing
and have wings.'

That night, Ella dangled a strand of wool over her grandma's new kittens.

'What does love look like?' said Ella.

'Oh, it's something like a dream, my dear,' said Ella's grandmother, who had warm hands and soft cheeks. 'Sweet dreams all day and night.'

Ella watched the kittens curl
into their mother's tummy.
She watched the light bounce
and sparkle in their eyes.

Then Ella had an idea.

'What is this kitten doing here?' said Mrs Gooseberry.

She looked up and down the street.

Ella crouched by the fence.
She could hear Mrs Gooseberry
talking quietly to the kitten.

Then Ella heard a soft purr and
the gentle click of a closing door.

The next day, Ella peeked
through her window.

Little paws patted at ripe tomatoes. Mrs Gooseberry hummed a song.

'Mrs Gooseberry has a sparkle in her eye today. Look, she's singing and dancing in her kitchen,' said Ella's mother.

In the weeks that followed, Ella watched Mrs Gooseberry do things she'd never seen her do.

It even seemed to Ella, that Mrs Gooseberry now liked her front yard almost as much as her backyard.

'Looks like Mrs Gooseberry has found love again,' said Ella.

'Sweet dreams Mrs Gooseberry.'